# Glenna's Seeds

Written by Nancy Edwards

Illustrated by Sarah K. Hoctor

Child & Family Press • Washington, DC

CWLA Press is an imprint of the Child Welfare League of America. The Child Welfare League of America is the nation's oldest and largest membership-based child welfare organization. We are committed to engaging people everywhere in promoting the well-being of children, youth, and their families, and protecting every child from harm.

CHILD WELFARE LEAGUE OF AMERICA, INC.
HEADQUARTERS
440 First Street, NW, Third Floor, Washington, DC 20001-2085
E-mail: books@cwla.org

CURRENT PRINTING (last digit)
10 9 8 7 6 5 4 3 2

Cover and text design by Sarah K. Hoctor

Printed in the United States of America

ISBN # 0–87868–788–2

*Library of Congress Cataloging-in-Publication Data*

Edwards, Nancy, 1952-
    Glenna's seeds/by Nancy Edwards; illustrated by Sarah Hoctor.
        p. cm.
    Summary: When Glenna gives away a packet of flower seeds, it sets off a chain of kind events among her neighbors.
    ISBN 0-87868-788-2
    [1. Seeds--Fiction. 2. Kindness--Fiction. 3. Neighborliness--Fiction.
4. Neighbors--Fiction.] I. Hoctor, Sarah K., ill.
PZ7.E2633 Gl  2001
[E]--dc21                                                    00-047401

To my Mom and Dad

*W*illow Street lay cold and silent in the afternoon sunshine.
Not a person could be seen.

From around the corner came the sound of skipping feet. Glenna and her friend Amy bounded onto Willow Street, side by side. Mr. Nordberg's dog barked hello.

Glenna clutched a packet of marigold seeds in one hand, a free sample from garden day at school. As she passed Miss Rose's house, she noticed an empty flower pot on her front step. Glenna dropped the packet of seeds into the pot. "A flower for a flower," she said to Amy, and they skipped on.

A few minutes later, Miss Rose drove
up. From her trunk she pulled a tray of
red geraniums. Setting the flowers
on her porch, she noticed the
seeds in the pot.

"I wonder," she said to herself. "If I plant marigolds in this pot, what will I do with my geraniums?" Miss Rose carefully planted and watered the seeds.

Then she picked up three
geraniums and carried them
down the street. She placed
one on Mrs. Robbins' front step,
one on Mrs. Sassanella's,
and one on Mr. Potter's.

Mrs. Robbins poked her head out her door and saw the flowers. She looked down the street and saw one just like it on Mrs. Sassanella's step. "What a sweet lady," she said. "And I know just what she'd like."

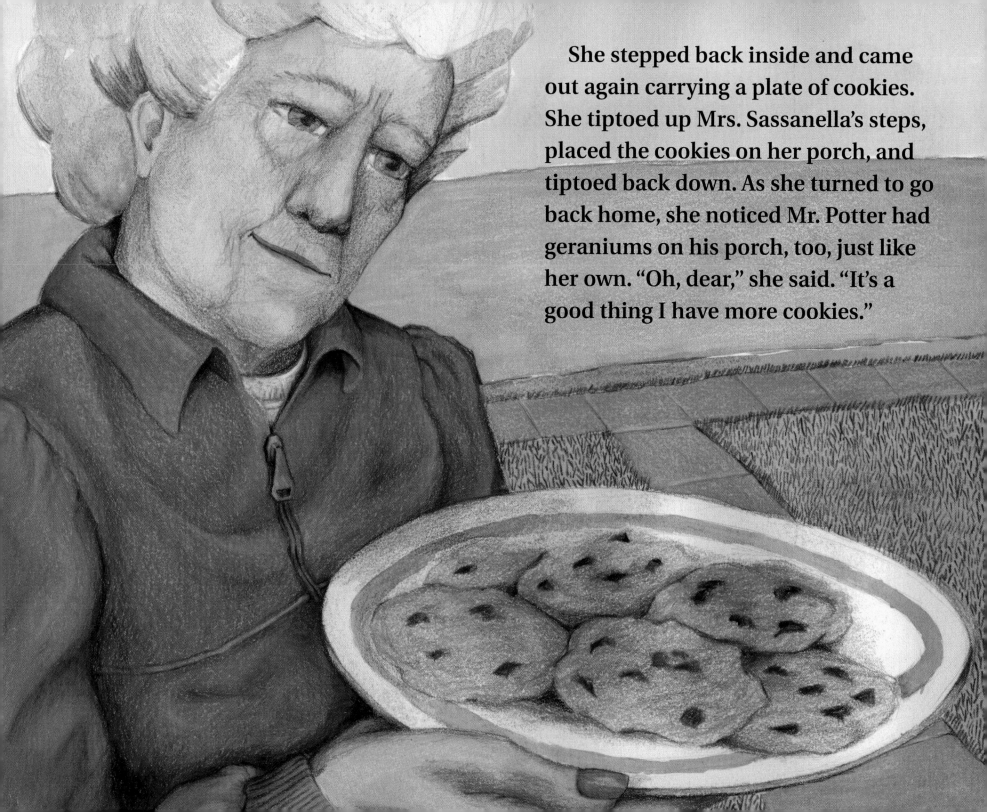

She stepped back inside and came out again carrying a plate of cookies. She tiptoed up Mrs. Sassanella's steps, placed the cookies on her porch, and tiptoed back down. As she turned to go back home, she noticed Mr. Potter had geraniums on his porch, too, just like her own. "Oh, dear," she said. "It's a good thing I have more cookies."

When Mr. Potter opened his door to get his newspaper, he saw a plate of cookies on his porch. "Oh, paperboy!" he called down the street.

Marty stopped his bike and turned to look. "Yes sir?"

"Did you see who brought me these cookies?"

Marty shook his head. "Maybe it was Mrs. Watson. It always smells like a bakery over there."

Marty pedaled on. When he reached Mrs. Watson's house, he left his bike on the sidewalk and carried her garbage can up to the house. He cast an interested glance toward the kitchen window.

"I see that nose of yours sniffing, Marty," Mrs. Watson called, laughing. "Come here. I've got something for your mom." She handed him a stack of magazines.

Marty slipped them into his newspaper bag.

"And this fudge is for you and your sister, Glenna," she added.

At the end of the block, Marty saw Glenna and Amy walking a dog. "You talked Mr. Nordberg into letting you walk his dog?" he asked.

"We like Star," Glenna said.

Marty handed one piece of fudge to
her and one to Amy. "More goodies
from Mrs. Watson," he explained.

Glenna and Amy ate their fudge as
slowly as they could
to make it last.

When they brought Star back to Mr. Nordberg's house, they found him next door, pulling weeds from Mrs. Sobaski's flower bed.

"Thanks a lot, girls," he said, taking the leash from their hands. "It gave me a little extra time, so I thought I'd do my good deed for the day."

The girls turned to leave. "Look," whispered Glenna. "Mrs. Sassanella's putting a loaf of bread on Mr. Nordberg's doorstep."

Mrs. Sassanella winked at the girls and put her finger to her lips.

Glenna said good-bye to Amy
and skipped all the way home, up
the steps, and to the door.

"Hi, sweetie," said Glenna's mother. "How was your day? Did anything good happen?"

"I got a packet of flower seeds at school," Glenna said, "but I gave it away to Miss Rose."

"That was a lovely thing to do," her mother said, bending down to give her a hug. "It's amazing, isn't it? So much can grow from a tiny packet of seeds."